AND THE EMPEROR OF ENVY

ZONDERKIDZ

Larryboy and the Emperor of Envy
Copyright © 2002 Big Idea, Inc. VEGGIETALES®, character names, likenesses and other indicia are trademarks of Big Idea, Inc. All rights reserved.

Requests for information should be addressed to:

Zonderkidz, *Grand Rapids, Michigan 49530*

Library of Congress Cataloging-in-Publication Data

Gaffney, Sean.
    Larryboy and the Emperor of Envy / written by Sean Gaffney.
        p. cm.
    "Big idea."
    "Based on the hit video series: Larryboy. Created by Phil Vischer. Series Adapted by
    Tom Bancroft."
    Summary: Larryboy, a heroic cucmber with plunger ears, comes to the rescue when the vegetable residents of Bumblyburg come down with bad cases of envy from slurping Slushees tainted by the diabolical Emperor of Envy.
    ISBN 978-0-310-70467-6
    [1. Heroes—Fiction. 2. Cucumbers—Fiction. 3. Vegetables —Fiction. 4. Envy—Fiction.]
I. Larryboy. II. Title.
    PZ7.G1194Lar 2002
    [Fic] — dc21

2002012696

Written by: Sean Gaffney
Editor: Cindy Kenney and Gwen Ellis
Cover and interior illustrations: Michael Moore
Cover design and art direction: Paul Conrad, Karen Poth, and Jody Langley
Interior design: Holli Leegwater, John Trent, and Karen Poth

Printed in the United States of America

11 12 13 14 15 16 17 18 19 20 21 /DCI/ 29 28 27 26 25 24 23 22 21 20 19 18 17

VeggieTales

LARRYBOY

AND THE EMPEROR OF ENVY

™

WRITTEN BY
SEAN GAFFNEY

ILLUSTRATED BY
MICHAEL MOORE

BASED ON THE HIT VIDEO SERIES: LARRYBOY
CREATED BY PHIL VISCHER
SERIES ADAPTED BY TOM BANCROFT

ZONDER**kidz**

ZONDERVAN.com/
AUTHORTRACKER
follow your favorite authors

TABLE OF CONTENTS

A CONTENT HEART
IS A HEALTHY HEART.

A HEART AT PEACE
GIVES LIFE TO THE BODY,
BUT ENVY ROTS THE BONES.

–PROVERBS 14:30

CHAPTER 1

SOMETHING ROTTEN IN THE SCHOOL OF BUMBLYBURG

It was a typical day at Bumblyburg's Veggie Valley Elementary School. Well, okay, maybe it wasn't such a typical day. In fact, something just plain weird was going on. The teacher, Mr. Asparagus, was acting a bit oddly.

"Don't you think Mr. Asparagus is acting a bit oddly?" asked Lenny Carrot about his teacher.

"He sure is," said Laura Carrot. "And he looks kind of funny. Like cardboard."

"His lips don't move when he talks," Percy Pea piped in. "That's weird."

"You know," said Renee Blueberry, "he looks a bit like a scallion from the side."

"What do you think, Junior?" asked Laura.

Junior Asparagus didn't know what to think! After all, the teacher was his father. But his dad was acting oddly. And he sure did look funny. Almost as if he was wearing a cardboard mask drawn with crayon.

"Time for a math lesson," squeaked the teacher.

"See!" whispered Percy. "His lips didn't move!"

"That doesn't sound like my dad," said Junior.

The teacher put a black bag on top of his desk. "Now, children," the teacher said, "I want you all to put your milk money into this bag. Then we will play a game."

"What game?" asked Junior.

"Hide-and-Seek," replied the teacher. "You will close your eyes and count to a million while I run and hide. Won't that be fun?"

Junior thought hard. His dad sounded funny, looked as if he was wearing a cardboard mask, talked without moving his lips, and now asked the kids to hand over their milk money for a game of Hide-and-Seek.

"Hey!" shouted Junior. "You aren't my dad! You're the Milk Money Bandit!"

"But I look like your dad, don't you think?" asked the teacher.

"I think you're wearing a mask," said Junior.

"Am not," said the teacher.

"Are too!"

"Am not!"

That moment, a rather large suction cup flew through the open window and plopped onto Mr. Asparagus' face. With a loud *THWOOP*, the plunger was pulled back through the window, ripping off the mask. It was the Milk Money Bandit after all!

"Erk!" shrieked the Bandit.

"I knew it!" exclaimed Junior. "But where did that

plunger come from?"

All the students turned and looked out the window. It was Larryboy! One of his suction-cup ears sported the Milk Money Bandit's mask, and he was trying to shake it loose.

"I am that hero!" Larryboy proclaimed.

Then Larryboy leaped through the open window, tripped on the windowsill, and fell into the classroom, landing on his face.

"I meant to do that," the hero said, popping upright. "Now, Bandit, where is the *real* Mr. Asparagus? Talk now, unless you want the other ear!"

Larryboy leaned threateningly toward the bandit.

"No, not the ears! I'll talk!" howled the villain. "I just wish I had more milk money!"

Larryboy scowled at the bandit.

"Mr. Asparagus is in the closet!" the bandit said, quickly.

Junior ran to the closet and opened the door.

"Dad!"

"Son!"

Junior's dad hopped out of the closet.

"It sure was dark in there," Mr. Asparagus said. "Thank you, Junior."

Mr. Asparagus came out of the closet and looked at the Milk Money Bandit quite sternly. "*You* should learn to be content with the money you have!" he scolded. "Thank *you*, Larryboy, for saving the day!"

Larryboy smiled. "My pleasure," he said. "And now to take care of the bandit!"

CHAPTER 2

I AM THAT HERO!

A short while later, Chief Croswell arrived at the classroom.

"I understand the Milk Money Bandit is ready to be taken to jail," he said.

"As soon as he is done at the blackboard," Larryboy responded.

The bandit was at the board, writing "I will not steal milk money" one thousand times.

"A fitting punishment for his crime," the Chief said.

"And now, my work here is done!" said Larryboy. He jumped out the window, tripping on the sill again, and fell onto the lawn.

"I meant to do that," the hero said as he popped back up.

Then Larryboy hopped into the Larry-Mobile and sped off toward his secret hideout.

Soon, the videophone in the Larry-Mobile began chirping.

"Hello, Archie," said Larryboy. Archibald—Larryboy's assistant, manservant, and technical wizard—appeared on the video screen.

"Well done, Larryboy!" Archibald said. "I monitored the whole thing from the Larry-Cave. You did splendidly."

"Thank you," said Larryboy.

"However, you may wish to be more careful jumping through windows."

"I think my mask throws off my depth perception."

"Well, never mind that now. I called to remind you of

tonight's superhero class."

"Tonight? But tonight is a classic double-feature night at the movies!"

"Well," said Archibald, "what do you think is more important, attending movies or school?"

"But the movies are *Attack of the Rotten Tomato* plus *Salad Wars: Frankencelery Strikes Back*!" exclaimed Larryboy.

Archibald glared at Larryboy through the screen.

"I'm on my way to school! Over and out!" Our hero spun his roadster around and zoomed down the street.

CHAPTER 3

A TYPICAL NIGHT IN SUPERHERO SCHOOL

Larryboy raced down the hallway of the Bumblyburg Community College, stopping in front of a door with a big sign that read, "Superhero 101: The Basics of Being Super."

"Here it is," Larryboy mumbled to himself. "I hope I'm not late."

Our hero stuck his head inside the doorway. The classroom was filled with superheroes, all sitting and facing the front. Bok Choy, the professor, stood in the front of the class. Larryboy slipped in, hoping not to be noticed. Unfortunately, he also tripped over the Norse superhero's backpack and toppled over a chair.

"Let me interrupt class with a riddle," said Bok Choy. "What do these three things have in common: an overdue library book, a school bus that is behind schedule, and Larryboy? Would the cucumber in the back like to guess?"

"Uhm," sputtered Larryboy.

"They are all *late!*" pronounced his teacher.

"That's a good riddle!" Larryboy said. "What's black, white, and read all over?"

Bok Choy took a deep breath and stared at Larryboy.

"Sorry, I was trying to slip in unnoticed."

"Slip in unnoticed?" Bok Choy asked. "A large cucumber dressed in yellow, sporting a big purple cape, and bumping into chairs in the back row? It's a wonder you were noticed at all. Take your seat, and try not to be late again."

Larryboy slipped into a chair. Bok Choy resumed his lecture.

"As I was saying, envy is a dangerous thing—especially to a superhero! Let's look at this chart showing the effects

of envy on the super body."

Larryboy looked at the superhero sitting next to him. He was a decorated apple, dressed in red, white, and blue. The headdress covering his head had two small wings attached. He also had a marvelous round shield that was painted blue with a big white *A* in the middle.

"Psst," whispered Larryboy. "Howdy. I'm Larryboy, from Bumblyburg. Who are you?"

"American Pie, defender of truth, justice, and vitamin A," American Pie whispered back. "I'm from Tiggety Town. What's the answer to *your* riddle?"

"Oh, that's easy! A Larryboy chapter book!"

"Huh?" American Pie asked curiously.

"Never mind," Larryboy said. "Hey! I sure like the wings on your head. Can you fly?"

"Nope," said the captain. "But they do make me look cool."

"Nifty," said Larryboy.

"Moving right along," Bok Choy urged with authority as he cleared his throat to demand more attention. "I want you all to take out your *Superhero Handbooks* and turn to section 20, paragraph 14, line 30."

"Psst!" Larryboy whispered to American Pie. "Can I look on with you? I left my *Superhero Handbook* in my glove compartment."

"Sure," said his neighbor.

"The book says, 'A heart at peace gives life to the body, but envy rots the bones,'" read Bok Choy. "Envy, also known as jealousy, eats away at you from the inside. It is an evil to avoid!"

Larryboy couldn't concentrate. He kept staring at American Pie's shield.

"That's a really nifty shield," he whispered.

"Thanks," American Pie whispered back.

"Can I hold it for a minute?" asked our hero.

"Okay," said the Pie. "Just be very careful."

Larryboy took the shield. It was heavier than it looked.

"Neat-o," said Larryboy.

"There is only one cure for envy," Bok Choy continued with his lecture. "You must learn to be happy with the things you already have. Instead of wishing you had your neighbor's car, be grateful for your own car. Instead of desiring your neighbor's cat, think of how happy you are with your own dog."

"What if I don't have a dog?" asked the Scarlet Tomato.

"I was just using that as an example," explained Bok Choy.

"My neighbor has a dog," said the tomato. "But I don't."

Bok Choy sighed.

"What do *you* have?" asked the teacher.

"A goldfish."

"Can you be content with that?"

"Sure. It's a pretty good goldfish."

"All right then," the teacher continued. "Remember, a content heart is a healthy heart. Repeat that, heroes."

"A content heart is a healthy heart," the class members

repeated—except for Larryboy. He was busy playing with the shield.

Larryboy lifted the disk up and down, playing with the weight in his hands.

"Psst," he whispered. "I bet you can throw this shield about a mile!"

"Perhaps," agreed American Pie. "But not in *here!*"

"It would make a great Frisbee," Larryboy said as he pretended to throw the shield like a Frisbee.

"Be careful!" hissed American Pie.

"Don't worry," said Larryboy. "I'm always careful… oops."

Larryboy wasn't holding on tightly enough. The shield flew around the room, careening off one wall only to ricochet off another.

"What's going on?" demanded Bok Choy.

"Look out!" shouted Electro-Melon.

"My shield!" yelled American Pie.

"Ahhh!" screamed Bok Choy as the shield bounced
to the front of the room, heading straight for him.

He raised the *Superhero Handbook* to block the
flying disk. The shield skimmed over the edge of the book
and shot through Bok Choy's head, giving him a flattop.
The whole class stared at their instructor
for a moment. Finally, Bok Choy broke the silence.

"Class, it looks like Larryboy is more interested in a
different lesson," he said. "It seems he would rather
practice being a barber!"

"Oops," said Larryboy.

CHAPTER 4

ENTER ... THE EMPEROR

Meanwhile, in a secret hideaway on the edge of Bumblyburg, an evil plan was being designed. Not just any evil plan, mind you, but that of Larryboy's nemesis, the Emperor Napoleon of Crime and Other Bad Stuff! The evil cherry tomato was sitting in his throne room when he called in his soldiers.

"Troops! Come in here!" called the villain.

The Emperor's army stumbled into the room. The term *army*, as it turns out, was a bit misleading. In fact, this particular army was really two muscular sweet potatoes named Frank and Jesse.

"And we really aren't that sweet," said Jesse.

"Who are you talking to?" asked Frank.

"Nobody," Jesse responded.

"Listen up, soldiers!"

barked the Emperor. "It's time for me to share with you my plan to conquer all of Bumblyburg!"

"How sweet! I always wished we could do something like that," Jesse exclaimed.

"I've managed to get my hands on a very special formula," the Emperor said. "I call it the Envy Formula!"

With a flourish, the Emperor waved a flask of blue liquid in front of the sweet potatoes.

"Gee, I wish I had an envy formula," Jesse commented.

"I wish *you'd* be quiet!" said Frank.

"Anyone who drinks this formula will be filled with envy. And we all know that envy makes people weak. But with *this* formula, they become super weak," the Emperor continued. "And I plan to see to it that everyone in Bumblyburg gets a taste!"

"That's nice," said Jesse. "Sharing like that is a real nice thing."

"Let me get this straight," said Frank. "Drinking the formula makes a person jealous; and when they get jealous, they get super weak?"

"That's right," answered the villain. "And the more envious they are, the weaker they become! They will feel tired and sluggish. They will hardly be able to move. They will only want to lie down and rest!"

"You know, I'm kind of tired myself," said Jesse.

"Didn't you take a nap this afternoon?" asked Frank.

"Yes, but only a little one."

"Can we get back to the point, please," demanded the

Emperor. "Now then, are there any other questions?"

"Yes," Jesse said. "Are you *really* a tomato?"

The Emperor let out a growl. "Yes, I am a tomato!"

"But aren't you too small to be a tomato?" Jesse asked.

"I've explained this a million times!" the Emperor ranted. "I am a cherry tomato. We are *supposed* to be small."

"So doesn't that make you more of a fruit than a tomato?" asked Jesse.

"Actually," Frank interrupted, "from a strictly scientific standpoint, tomatoes are fruits and not vegetables."

"Really?" asked Jesse. "I don't think I knew that."

"Quiet!" shouted the Emperor. "Are there any more questions about the formula?"

"I have one," said Frank. "How does the formula help us take over Bumblyburg?"

"Simple," the Emperor replied. "Once everyone has taken the formula, they will become envious. When they become envious, they will become weak. And then they will have no strength left to fight us when we take over Bumblyburg! Bwaa-haa-haa-ha!" The Emperor threw back his head and laughed. Frank and Jesse laughed too, although Jesse later admitted he didn't really get the joke.

CHAPTER 5

NEXT DAY AT THE BUMBLE

The next day at the *Daily Bumble*, Bob the editor was fuming mad. "I'm fuming mad," said Bob.

He was talking to Vicki, the staff photographer. Junior, the cub reporter from Veggie Valley Elementary School, listened in.

"What's got your goat this time, Chief?" asked Vicki. She liked to tease Bob by calling him "Chief." She knew that got his goat. Bob ignored it.

"Mister Slushee, Bumblyburg's very own ice cream shop, is having a Slushee-Slurping contest today," Bob grumbled. "They are giving out free Slushees to the whole town. It will be a major event!"

"Sounds good to me," said Vicki. "So what's your beef?"

"What's my beef? I don't have an available reporter to cover the story, so I have to go myself. I wish I had a reporter available."

"That's not so bad," said Vicki. "I'm going to be there to take photographs."

"But I don't *like* Slushees!" said Bob.

"What's not to like about Slushees?" asked Vicki.

"I get brain-freeze headaches," said Bob.

"Excuse me," Junior cleared his throat. "But I could report on the contest."

"Who's that?" demanded Bob.

"Me, Junior Asparagus, sir!"

"Oh, you," said Bob. "Listen kid, it's great that you're the cub reporter covering stories from Veggie Valley Elementary School, but you're just a kid. You can't cover important stories like the Mister Slushee's Slushee-Slurping Contest. Understand?"

Junior nodded.

"What are you doing here, anyway?" asked the editor.

"I'm turning in my front-page story on Larryboy's capture of the Milk Money Bandit," Junior replied.

Everyone suddenly heard a loud beep, much like that of a microwave oven. Bob looked to the corner of the office where Larry, the janitor, was mopping.

"I didn't notice you there," said Bob.

"Excuse me, but I think your mop is beeping," said Junior.

"Time to mop the closet," Larry said, dashing out of the room.

"Did that cucumber have a timer in his mop?" asked Bob.

"Now *that's* keeping to a tight cleaning schedule!" marveled Vicki.

CHAPTER 6

ARCHIE CALLING

Larry quickly ducked into the hall closet. After checking to make sure he was alone, he stuck his head into the mop. The seemingly plain mop had a video screen built into the strands. Archibald appeared on the screen.

"Hello, Archie," said Larry.

"Greetings, Master Larry," said Archibald. "How is your job at the newspaper?"

"I'm glad you brought that up," said Larry. "I still don't understand why I have to be a janitor. I am a world-famous superhero!"

That was true. For Larry, the janitor, was also Larryboy, the superhero!

"Let me explain it again," said his trusted friend. "By working at the newspaper, you can learn about criminal activity the moment it is reported."

"Couldn't I just watch BNN, the Bumblyburg News Network?"

"And sit around the house all day?" asked Archibald. "No,

being at the *Bumble* is much better."

"Sounds like you are trying to get me out of the house," Larry laughed.

"Maybe we should change the subject," Archibald quickly interrupted. "I have important information for you!"

"Me too!" said Larry excitedly. "I learned something really important while cleaning the editor's office."

"I told you the janitor job would pay off," said Archibald. "What did you learn?"

"They're giving out free Slushees at Mister Slushee today!"

"Oh, I see," said his partner.

"So what's *your* important information?" asked Larry.

"I wanted to warn you that your archenemy, Emperor Napoleon of Crime and Other Bad Stuff, has been spotted near Bumblyburg."

"The Emperor near Bumblyburg? That *is* important news. How did you hear about it?"

"Well, er..." said Archibald. "Actually, I saw it on BNN."

"Hmmm," said Larry. "Well, I had better make plans to deal with the Emperor. And you know what helps a cucumber make good plans?"

"What?" asked Archibald.

"Free Slushees! Toodles!"

Larry clicked off the videophone and pulled the mop off of his head. Whistling, he stepped out of the closet and bounded down the hall. Junior and Vicki were passing by the closet.

"It sounded like the janitor was mumbling to himself in the closet," said Junior.

"He is a strange one," said Vicki. "But he sure is good with a plunger!"

CHAPTER 7

THE PLOT
(AND THE SLUSHEE) THICKENS

It was pandemonium outside Mister Slushee. It seemed as if the entire town was trying to get in for their free Slushees! Chief Croswell blocked the door.

"Hold on, everyone," he said. "You know that Mister Slushee doesn't open for business for another ten minutes. Until that time, we can't let anybody in."

"Ohhhhh!" groaned the crowd.

The Emperor and his henchmen were hiding in the alley next to the Slushee shop.

"Did you hear that?" asked Frank. "With Chief Croswell blocking the door, we can't get into the shop so we can pour the Envy Formula into the Slushee machine, thus ensuring that everyone in Bumblyburg drinks the formula!"

"Good job at bringing the reader up to speed," said Jesse.

"What reader?" asked Frank.

"Never mind that," said the Emperor. "I can get past Chief Croswell. You two stand next to the back door."

"But the door is locked," said Frank.

"I know that," said the Emperor. "I will unlock it from the inside."

"But how will you get past Chief Croswell?" asked Jesse.

"I will use my superpower!" declared the cherry tomato.

"Cool," said Jesse.

"Neat," said Frank.

"What superpower?" asked Jesse.

The Emperor shook his head.

"Weren't you paying attention in supervillain school?" he asked. "All supervillains are either mad geniuses or have superpowers."

"What kind of powers?" asked Frank.

"You know," said the Emperor. "Like super strength, or super speed, or the ability to fly."

"Wow! What's your superpower?"

"When I hold my breath," explained the villain, "I become very, very small."

"You're already are very, very small," said Jesse.

"I become even smaller!" yelled the Emperor. "Watch!"

The Emperor held his breath. Then he began shrinking! Soon he was almost too small to see.

"That *is* small," said Jesse.

"You said it," agreed Frank.

The Emperor let out his breath and grew back to normal size.

"When I'm tiny, I can slip right past Chief Croswell

without being seen."

"You can usually slip by most people without being seen," Jesse observed.

The Emperor growled and said, "Go stand by the back door and wait for me!"

Then he held his breath and shrunk down to a miniscule size. He hopped around the corner and headed for the shop's front door. Chief Croswell was a giant from his point of view!

The Emperor easily slid through underneath the door and into the shop. Once inside, he let out his breath. Back to full size, he gleefully ran and opened the back door.

"Get in here," he said to his henchmen.

Frank and Jesse lumbered into the shop. The Emperor made his way to the Slushee machine. He took out the vial of blue liquid.

"Now, if one of you would be so kind as to pour this vial into the Slushee machine," he said, "then when everyone eats their free Slushees, they will be infected with the Envy Formula!"

"Why don't *you* dump it in?" asked Jesse.

"I'm not tall enough to reach the opening," said the Emperor. "That's why I need your help."

"Why don't you grow back to full size?" asked Jesse.

"I *am* full size," barked the Emperor.

"Why don't I stop talking now," said Jesse.

"That would be a good idea!"

Frank took the vial from the Emperor and poured it into the Slushee machine.

"Good work!" said the Emperor. "Now, let's sneak out the back so no one will suspect a thing. Then all we need to do is wait until everyone has slurped a Slushee. At that moment, we can march on Bumblyburg!"

"Can we stop by my house first?" asked Jesse. "If we're going to be marching, I want to be wearing comfortable shoes."

"Just go!" yelled the Emperor.

Emperor Napoleon of Crime and Other Bad Stuff led his henchmen out the back door, laughing maniacally.

CHAPTER 8

THE SLUSHEE CONTEST

When Chief Croswell opened the doors, the citizens of Bumblyburg stampeded into the shop. Wally helped Herbert work the Slushee machine, pouring out Slushee after Slushee. The shop was packed with vegetables.

"You were right," Vicki said to Bob. "This is a big story."

"I can't believe all these people," Bob said.

"Why not, Chief?" asked Vicki.

"You'd have to be very silly to get this excited about a Slushee contest."

"Look, there's Larry, our janitor," Vicki said.

"My point is proven!"

Larry was sitting with Junior at the far end of the counter.

"This is exciting," said Junior.

"Free Slushees!" said Larry.

"It looks like the whole town is here," said Junior.

"Free Slushees!" said Larry.

"I bet I could write a great story about this," said Junior. "Even if *some* people think I'm not grown up enough to be a real reporter."

"Free Slushees!" responded Larry.

"My dad says God made me special, just the way I am— and that I'll be grown up when I'm good and ready," Junior said. "But I want to be a grown-up right now!"

"Free Slushees!" said Larry.

Chief Croswell hopped onto the counter and tried to get everyone's attention.

"Attention!" he shouted.

Wally let out a loud whistle, and everyone quieted down.

"Thank you, Wally," said the chief. "Welcome to Mister Slushee's Slushee-Slurping Contest. I have been asked to officiate today's event."

"What's 'o-fish-he-ate'?" asked Larry.

"'O-fish-she-ate.' It means 'judge,'" said Junior.

"Poor fish," said Larry.

"Everyone who wants to compete must sit at the counter," explained the chief.

Herbert and Wally had finished filling up the counter with cup after cup of Slushee. They moved away from the Slushee machine and squeezed into two chairs. Larry and Junior already had seats, as did Officers Boysen and Blue, Laura, Lenny, and several others.

"You should compete!" encouraged Vicki.

"Don't be silly," said Bob.

"It's a great idea," Vicki said, with a wink. "Get a first-hand angle for the story."

"But I always get a brain freeze," Bob complained.

"Come on," Vicki teased. "A little Slushee isn't going to hurt you. Besides, if you eat it slowly enough, you won't get a headache."

"Eat slowly in a slurping contest?"

"Get up there, big guy." Vicki nudged Bob up to the counter.

"Okay, contestants," announced Chief Croswell. "When I say, 'Go,' grab a Slushee cup and start slurping! When you finish a cup, take another. When this alarm clock beeps, the contest will be over! Any questions?"

"Where are the straws?" asked Bob.

Laughter rang through the shop.

"There are no straws in a Mister Slushee Slushee-Slurping Contest," explained the chief. "Just stick your face into the Slushee and slurp."

"But isn't that a little messy?" asked Bob.

"Ready?" asked the chief.

"Couldn't I at least get a spoon?" moaned Bob.

"Set," the chief called.

"This is so embarrassing," said Bob.

"Slurp!" shouted Chief Croswell.

The contestants stuck their faces into their Slushee cups. Bob sighed, pursed his lips, puckered up, and put his face to a cup.

"While they race, the rest of us also get to enjoy Slushees too" said Chief Croswell. "Free Slushees for everyone!"

The chief hopped to the back of the counter and started filling Slushee cups. He passed the cups around until everyone in the shop was busy slurping.

CHAPTER 9

TEN MINUTES LATER, OR "I DON'T BELIEVE I SLURPED THE WHOLE THING!"

BEEP!

The alarm clock on the counter went off. Larry's head shot up.

"Hello, Archie?" he said.

"Time!" Chief Croswell called out.

The contestants lifted their heads from their Slushees. They all had multicolored stains on their faces. Chief Croswell moved down the counter, counting empty Slushee cups.

"Five Slushees for Larry! Three for Junior! Six for the Berry brothers, Officers Boysen and Blue!"

The Berry brothers smiled a raspberry-strawberry and banana-grape smile.

"Only one for Bob," announced Chief Croswell.

"And I still got a headache," he grumbled.

"Sixteen for Herbert!"

"Sixteen?" asked Larry. "That's a lot of Slushee!"

"Wait," said Chief Croswell. Wally might have more empty cups."

The chief counted and then recounted, holding

each cup up to make sure it was empty.

"Seventeen cups! Wally wins!"

"Hooray!" shouted the crowd.

"Urp!" belched Wally.

The chief pulled a large trophy from behind the counter.

"Wally, in honor of your amazing appetite, I award you this Mister Slushee Slushee–Slurping Trophy!"

He handed the trophy to Wally.

"I wish I had a big trophy like Wally," said Herbert.

"Me too," said Officers Boysen and Blue.

"I would be much happier with a trophy like his," said

Officer Blue.

"Not as happy as *I* would be!" insisted Officer Boysen.

"You know what would make *me* happier?" asked Bob. "If I had a lot of reporters on my staff, like all the big-town papers have."

"Where did that come from?" asked Vicki.

"I don't know," said Bob. "It just came out."

"Well, come to think of it," Vicki continued, "I would be happier if I had a brand-new digital camera, like the big-shot photographers have."

Suddenly everybody started talking at once.

"I wish I had a pony, like Margo has," said Laura.

"I want Harry's new Larryboy action figure," said Lenny.

"I wish I was grown up like, well, like grown-ups," whined Junior.

The whole shop was full of "I wish" and "I want" and "I'd rather." Envy was filling the shop! Suddenly, the door burst open and a loud laugh was heard. The crowd shushed and turned to the door. There, in the doorway, they saw ...

Nothing.

CHAPTER 10

THE EMPEROR'S ENTRANCE

"Down here! I'm down here!"

Everyone shifted their gaze down and saw the Emperor standing on the threshold!

"I have come to take over Bumblyburg," announced the Emperor.

The crowd looked at the small menace and began laughing.

"Oh, yeah?" said Chief Croswell. "You and what army?"

"Me and this army," said the villain as he stepped aside to make room for his henchmen.

Frank and Jesse lumbered in through the door.

"*Those* two? *They're* your army?" chuckled Bob.

Everyone laughed again.

"Officers Boysen and Blue," said Chief Croswell, "take these scoundrels into custody."

"I wish I had an army

like you have," said Officer Blue.

"Even a couple of deputies would be nice," agreed Officer Boysen.

"Boysen! Blue!" snapped the chief.

"Right! You are all under arrest!" Officer Blue pronounced. But as he stepped forward, he stumbled and fell to the floor, with Office Boysen stumbling right behind him.

"What's wrong with the Berry brothers?" asked Junior.

"I don't know," said a stunned Officer Boysen.

"I don't feel very good," Blue mumbled from the floor.

"I don't feel very good either," said Herbert.

"Do you think it's from slurping too many Slushees?" asked Wally.

"You can *never* have too many Slushees," Herbert replied.

"Hah!" gloated the Emperor. "You are all too weak to stand up to me! You laugh at my height! You laugh at my army! Well, who's laughing now?"

"You are, boss," said Jesse.

"I know I am. That's my point."

"Oh."

"To make sure no one interferes, my troops will tuck you all safely away in jail. Then Bumblyburg will be mine! While you sit in jail wishing for things you can't have, I am going to make all *my* wishes come true!"

"Wait!" said Chief Croswell weakly. "Aren't you forgetting about Larryboy? When he hears about this, you will be sorry!"

At the far end of the counter, Larry began thinking.

I wish I *was Larryboy,* he mused to himself. "Wait a minute. I am that hero!"

Larry hopped off his chair and snuck out through the back door.

CHAPTER 11

GOOD BATTLES EVIL

"Stop, vile villain!" Larryboy shouted.

He had reemerged from the back alley.

He was now dressed in his full Larryboy costume. The Emperor and his henchmen froze.

"What do we do now?" asked Jesse.

"He doesn't look weak," said Frank. "What if he didn't have any Slushees?"

The Emperor looked worried for a moment. Then he smiled.

"Look at his face, boys," he said.

Larryboy had a red-purple-green Slushee stain around his mouth!

"Okay, superhero," the Emperor said. "You got me. Before you take me in, may I ask you a question?"

"Sure," said Larryboy.

"Isn't there anything that someone else has that you wish you had?" asked the villain. "Like a toy, or a car, or a special skill?"

"A kitty-cat, maybe?" suggested Frank.

"Or an octopus?" added Jesse.

"Octopus?" asked Frank.

"I like octopuses," said Jesse.

"Don't you mean octopi?" asked Frank.

"No thanks," said Jesse. "I don't like pie. But I do wish I had a piece of cake."

"Gentlemen, please!" shouted the Emperor. "Well, Larryboy? Can't you think of anything?"

Larryboy thought for a moment.

"Now that you mention it," he said, "I would like to have a shield like American Pie has. That was nifty. Round and sturdy. And boy, that thing could fly!"

"Ahem." Vicki cleared her throat. "Larryboy, aren't you

in the middle of doing something important?"

"That's right," said Larryboy. "Okay, villains, let's go!"

"I've changed my mind," smirked the Emperor. "You will have to take us by force."

"Alright, if that's the way you want it."

Larryboy stepped forward, cocked his head, and let fly a mighty super-suction ear!

Only the ear didn't fly. It fizzled, actually, and fell to the floor at Larryboy's feet.

"I feel funny," the hero said. "And I'm too weak to shoot my ears right!"

The Emperor laughed. And laughed. And laughed.

CHAPTER 12

NINETY-NINE BOTTLES
OF SLUSHEE ON THE WALL

"In you go," said Jesse.

The Emperor's henchmen were escorting Herbert and Wally into a cell at the Bumblyburg prison.

"That's the last of them," said Frank. "The whole town, all in jail."

"Can't we at least have something to drink? I want something to drink!" whined Officers Boysen and Blue.

"There's ninety-nine bottles of Slushee on the wall," Frank pointed out.

"Yeah. Just take one down, pass it around," added Jesse.

"Ninety-eight bottles of Slushee on the wall," finished Frank.

"Hey, that would make a great song!" Jesse realized.

"Hey, sweet potato!"

Wally was yelling at them through the bars. He and Herbert were both sitting on the cots in the cell.

"Tell Herbert to give me his cot," Wally yelled. "It's softer than mine!"

"I'm too tired to switch cots," said Herbert. "Besides, I want his cot. It's firmer than mine!"

"Boy, I hope that Envy Formula wears off soon," said Frank. "These gourds are driving me crazy!"

The two henchmen walked out of the prison. A few cells down, Bob, Junior and Larryboy were sharing a cell.

"I feel super weak," Junior said.

"Me too," said Bob. "And my head hurts."

"Well," said Larryboy, "I feel weak, my head hurts, and

there is a ringing in my ears."

"That's because your ears *are* ringing," said Bob.

"They are?" Larryboy sat up on his cot. "Hello? Archie, is that you?"

"Hello, Larryboy!"

Larryboy could hear Archibald's voice through the radio set in his headdress. Bob and Junior, who couldn't

hear Archibald, looked on confused.

"Archie, am I glad to hear your voice," said Larryboy. "I'm in jail!"

"Oh, no," said Archibald. "I told you to slow down when driving through town!"

"It's not that," said Larryboy. "It's Emperor Napoleon of Crime and Other Bad Stuff!"

"Why are you telling *us* that?" asked Bob.

"I'm not talking to you," said Larryboy.

"You're not talking to me?" asked Archie.

"Yes, I'm talking to you," said Larryboy. "I'm not talking to Bob."

"Are you talking to *me*?" asked Junior.

"No, I'm talking to Archie," said the superhero.

Bob and Junior looked around the cell.

"He must be invisible," said Bob.

"I wish I had an invisible friend," said Junior.

"Archie isn't invisible," explained Larryboy. "You just can't see him."

"I wish I had a friend who wasn't invisible but you just couldn't see him," said Junior.

"Never mind explaining," Archibald pushed on. "Just tell me what happened."

So Larryboy told Archibald about the Mister Slushee Slushee-Slurping Contest, the Emperor's entrance, Officers Boysen and Blue becoming ill, and his own brief battle with the villain.

"And that's how we ended up here," said Larryboy.

"It's unbelievable, but I'm too weak to try to escape! I wish I was back home, like you."

"Keep your courage up, my friend," said Archibald. "I will go down to Mister Slushee and investigate. Maybe I can find out what is making so many people lose their strength!"

"Good idea, Archie," said Larryboy. "And while you're doing that, I'm going to lie down on my cot and dream that I had a mattress that wasn't lumpy. Over and out."

Larryboy sunk down on his cot and commenced dreaming.

CHAPTER 13

THE EMPEROR'S NEW BUMBLYBURG

"Lower!" shouted the Emperor.

The evil cherry tomato was standing in the large doorway to the Mister Slushee shop.

"I said lower!" he yelled again.

A loud **CRUNCH** rang out. Suddenly, the doorway to Mister Slushee was the ideal size for the short villain!

"That's perfect," said the Emperor. "Now on to the next building!"

Frank and Jesse stood next to the crank of a really huge, super gigantic, massively gargantuan vise grip. The vise was clamped down on the Mister Slushee shop. They had scrunched down the entire building to fit the Emperor!

"And it was really hard work," Jesse said.

"What was really hard work?" asked Frank.

"Scrunching down the entire building to fit the Emperor," said Jesse.

"What are you telling me for?" asked Frank.

"I know it was really hard work. I stood right here and scrunched with you."

"I'm not telling you," Jesse said. "I'm telling the reader."

"Oh … right!"

"Come along, men," the Emperor called. "We have a lot more scrunching to do!"

Frank and Jesse marched away from the Mister Slushee shop.

"Now that the buildings are being scrunched down to the Emperor's size," said Jesse, "how will *we* be able to stand up in them?"

"Quiet," said Frank. "Or the Emperor might decide to scrunch us down, too!"

As they left, Archibald tiptoed around the corner, wriggled his way through the door, and crawled into the building.

CHAPTER 14

ALFRED REPORTS BACK

BRRRING! BRRRING!

Larryboy sat up on his cot.

"Am I late for work again?" he asked.

"It's your ears," said Bob. "They're ringing again."

"Oh, excuse me," Larryboy said. "That's my radio hidden in my super-suction ears."

"I wish I had a radio," said Bob.

"I wish I had super-suction ears," said Junior.

"I wish I had a radio *and* super-suction ears!" exclaimed Larryboy.

"*You do*," Bob reminded him. "And they're still ringing.

"Right," said Larryboy. "Hello, Alfred?"

"Larryboy, I found something interesting. I took a very interesting sample from the Slushee machine."

"I wish I had a Slushee," said Larryboy. "Did it taste good?"

"I didn't eat it," said Archibald. "I

took it to the lab and ran some tests. The Slushees were tainted with what appears to be an envy formula."

"An envy formula," repeated Larryboy.

"What's he saying?" asked Bob.

"The Slushees were tainted with an envy formula," said the superhero. "I seem to recall someone talking about envy recently. If only I could remember where."

"Was it someone at Mister Slushee?" asked Archibald.

"How about someone you passed on the street?" asked Junior.

"Was it a used-car salesman?" suggested Bob.

"No, none of those."

"At the Veggie Valley Elementary School," Junior said, "our teacher once taught us about envy."

"That's it!" shouted Larryboy. "School!"

"You go to the Veggie Valley Elementary School, too?" asked Junior.

"No, but in my night class, Professor Bok Choy talked about envy. He said that envy rots the bones."

"There did seem to be a lot of jealousy at Mister Slushee," said Junior. "And after everyone became envious, we all started to feel weak. Envy caused our weakness!"

"I wish I had thought of that," said Bob.

"That's it!" said Archibald. "And God doesn't want us to be envious of others! No wonder you couldn't fight the Emperor!"

"So what do I do? What do I do?" asked Larryboy.

"To counteract the formula, you must stop being envious," said Archibald. "Then your strength will return."

"I can do that! Then I'll take care of the Emperor and his cronies. But how will I get out of this cell?"

"I wish I had the keys to this cell," said Junior.

"Of course, the keys!" Larryboy exclaimed.

"Why not just use your super-suction ears to get them?" asked Bob as they all gazed at the set of keys hanging on the far wall outside of the cell.

"They're all the way across the room! I don't know if I have the strength to shoot my super-suction ears that far," moaned Larry.

"Larryboy," Archibald said over the radio. "Simply stop being envious, and then you should have enough power to reach them."

"Oh! Of course!" Larryboy agreed. "I am the happiest cucumber alive! I'm happy with everything I have! I'm happy just being ..."

"Larryboy, you have a job to do!" Archibald reminded him.

"Right! Over and out!"

Larryboy stood up and wiggled an ear between the bars. Then he took aim, and *POP!* The plunger zoomed across the room, sticking to the keys. With a whir, Larryboy reeled his plunger back in, dragging the keys to the cell.

The superhero turned to face his friends as he tried to yank the keys through the bars. But his ear jammed between the bars, causing him to fall to the floor.

"Oops! I think they're stuck!" he admitted.

Bob and Junior helped Larryboy pull his ear back through the bars to retrieve the keys. Quickly, he unlocked the cell door.

"I'm off to see the Emperor," he proclaimed. "Who's with me?"

"I wish I had your energy," Bob said, "but helping you with those keys zapped every bit I had. I'm still too weak to leave."

"Me too," said Junior.

"You will have to go alone, Master Larry," said Archibald. "Just remember, don't be envious!"

CHAPTER 15

IF AT FIRST YOU DON'T SUCCEED ...

SCRUNCH!

"A little lower!"

The Emperor was standing in the doorway to the Bumblyburg Bank. Frank and Jesse were working the crank of the really huge, super gigantic, massively gargantuan vise that now clamped the bank.

"Halt! Stop that!"

Larryboy was on the scene. He stood defiantly in the middle of the street, facing the bank.

"Oh, look boys," the Emperor chuckled. "Guess who escaped from his cell?"

"Oh, I love riddles," said Jesse. "Did Officers Boysen and Blue escape?"

"No!" grumbled the Emperor.

"Do you really like riddles?" Larryboy asked the sweet potatoes. "'Cuz I have a really good one. What's purple and white and read?..."

"It's Larryboy!" the Emperor interrupted.

"Can't you see?"

"I thought it might be a trick question," said Jesse.

"I wanted to hear the end of the riddle," added Frank.

"Army, attack!" ordered the Emperor.

Frank and Jesse abandoned the crank and headed right for Larryboy.

"Larryboy, can you hear me?" Archibald called through the radio set.

"Loud and clear," said the hero.

"This would be a good time to test the new weapon that I installed in your left super-suction ear."

"The Maypole Ear? But it's not May, it's October."

"That's quite alright, Master Larry. Use it anyway."

"Who's he talking to?" asked Jesse.

"I don't know," replied Frank. "But watch out, he's getting ready to launch a plunger!"

POP! Larryboy's left super-suction ear flew through the air and landed on the ground between the two henchmen.

"Ha! He missed," gloated Frank.

"Maybe," said Larryboy. "Maybe not."

"Uh, Frank," said Jesse. "The plunger is making noise."

Indeed, the plunger was whirring. Suddenly, a tall pole rose up out of the center of it.

"What's that?" asked Frank, staring up at the pole.

A small *POP* resounded from the top of the pole, and two smaller plungers dropped down near the sweet potatoes. *PLOP! PLOP!* The mini-plungers landed squarely on each henchman's head.

"I don't like the sound of this," said Frank.

"Hey, I'm flying!" said Jesse.

The mini-plungers were being reeled to the top of the pole, carrying Jesse and Frank along with them.

"Help!" called Jesse.

"We're stuck up here," yelled Frank.

"Works like a charm," said Larryboy.

"Thank you," said Archibald.

"And now for the big guy," said Larryboy, looking down at his small adversary. "I mean, the little guy."

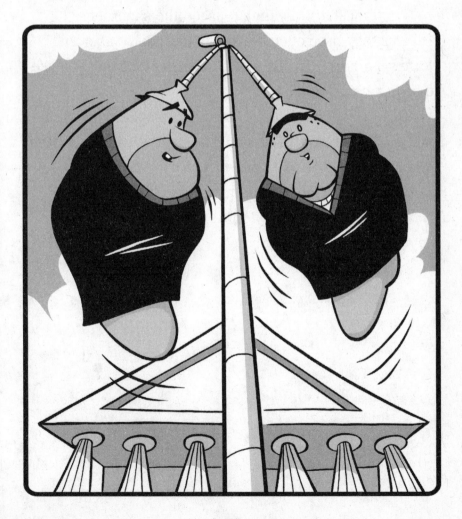

"Wait a minute," said the villain. "May I ask you something?"

"Oh no you don't!" said Larryboy.

"How about the shield that American Pie has? Wouldn't you like that?" taunted the Emperor.

"I'm not listening!" answered the superhero. "La, la, la, la, la, la, la!"

"Other superheroes can fly. Don't you wish you could fly?" the Emperor taunted.

"I'm not listen... fly, huh?" asked the superhero.

"Plus they have other wonderful toys. Remember that Norse superhero with the magic hammer? Wouldn't you like to have a hammer like him?"

"Gee, if I had a hammer," said Larryboy, "I could hammer in the morning. That would be cool. Why can't I have a hammer like that other superhero?"

Larryboy suddenly felt himself getting weaker.

"Oh, no!" he cried. "I don't know how to stay unenvious!"

CHAPTER 16

THE BUMBLYBURG PRISON BLUES

Back at the prison cell, Junior sat on his bunk in a bad mood.

"Hrumpf!" he cried.

"What's on your mind?" asked Bob.

"No matter how hard I try to not envy grown-ups, I don't feel any stronger," Junior replied. "I guess I just can't do it."

"Envy grown-ups?" Bob asked. "Why would you do something silly like that?"

"Grown-ups get to do all kinds of things that I can't. Like be real reporters. And stay up late. And eat nothing but macaroni and cheese for breakfast, lunch, and dinner."

"Still," reasoned Bob, "you get to do a lot of really cool things, too."

"Like what?" Junior was being a little grumpy.

"Well, you get to be cub reporter. Sure, I might not let you cover every story, but how many of the other kids you know get to have their stories published at all?"

"That's true," said Junior.

"And you get to play at recess. I haven't had recess since I was your age."

"Really?" asked Junior. "I do like recess."

"And you get to go to the movies for half-price. I can't go to the movies for half-price."

"My grandpa goes to the movies for half-price," replied Junior. "I bet it won't be long before you can, too."

"I'm *not* as old as your grandpa!" scowled Bob.

"You're not?" asked Junior.

"Let's change the subject," said Bob. "The point is, you can go to movies for half-price now."

"Yeah," said Junior. "I guess being a kid isn't so bad."

"More than that," said Bob. "Being Junior Asparagus isn't so bad."

"Yeah, I like being me!" agreed Junior. "Besides, I learned that little guys can do big things, too! I guess I was forgetting all about that! Hold it, I'm feeling stronger. In fact, I don't feel sick at all!"

"Really? That's probably because you

did more than stop being jealous. You were also content with what you have and who you are," Bob added.

"Yeah! The only way to really stop envy is by being content. A content heart is a healthy heart!" Junior pronounced.

"You said it, kid. And I'll print *that* in my paper any day!" Bob said.

"Oh, my! I'd better go," Junior shouted. "Larryboy doesn't know how to stop envy!"

CHAPTER 17
JUNIOR TO THE RESCUE

"Larryboy?"

"Yes, Archie?" Larryboy responded through his radio set.

"What is that strange sound I'm hearing?"

"What sound, Archie?"

"Well, it's sort of a scrunching and crunching sound."

"Oh, that," said Larryboy. "That would be my head."

"What?"

"Not now, Archie. I'm a little busy."

Larryboy was tied up and standing in the middle of the really huge, super gigantic, massively gargantuan vise. And the clamp was squeezing down on his head! Frank and Jesse had taken the vise off the bank, and they were now using it on Larryboy.

"Now you will know what it feels like to be short," the Emperor gloated.

"Is that what all this is about? *Your* wish to be tall? I don't suppose you would like to be stretched instead?" asked Larryboy.

"No."

"You really should consider it. Of course, you'd look more like a bell pepper. But you're always grouchy, so a pepper sorta suits you. I think you should consider it. Don't ya think?"

"Larryboy!" Junior was racing down the street toward the hero, yelling at the top of his lungs. It isn't enough to not be envious!"

"Hah!" said Jesse. "He learned that three chapters ago!"

"Could you guys hold it down for a second?" asked Larryboy. "I'm trying to hear Junior."

"Oh, sorry," said the sweet potatoes in unison.

"It's just like my dad said!" shouted Junior. "God made each of us special. And God wants us to be happy with who we are and what we have. That's how you defeat envy—by being content!"

"I can do that!" said Larryboy. "If I only knew what 'content' means."

"It means being happy with what you have, rather than wishing for things that others have!"

"Hey," said Jesse. "The kid's got a good point."

"Stop him!" yelled the Emperor. "He'll ruin everything!"

Frank, Jesse, and the Emperor ran toward Junior. The cub reporter spun around and darted the other way. But the potatoes and the Emperor were close behind.

"Help!" yelled Junior.

As they disappeared down the street, Larryboy was left

alone with his thoughts.

Be content, eh? Happy with what I have? Well, it is true that I don't have a cool shield. But I do have other nifty things, like super-suction ears. And I have Archie, who makes me cool stuff. And I get to live in Bumblyburg with some of the nicest vegetables you could ever hope to call friends. It is good to be Larryboy!

Larryboy stood up tall and proud. He flexed his cucumber muscles; and the ropes around him burst; and the really huge, super gigantic, massively gargantuan vise snapped in half!

"I AM THAT HERO!" Larryboy cried.

CHAPTER 18

TRY, TRY AGAIN

Down the street, Frank, Jesse, and the Emperor surrounded Junior.

"So," taunted the Emperor. "You think a little kid like yourself is going to outwit the Emperor?"

"I'm not so little," said Junior, defiantly. "I'm taller than you."

"He has a point there," agreed Jesse.

"Quiet!" shouted the Emperor. "Grab the kid, and let's get back to squishing Larryboy!"

"Did somebody mention my name?" Larryboy leaped into the middle of the gang, landing next to Junior.

"How did you escape from the vise?" asked Frank.

"Never mind that," said the Emperor. "It won't take much

to make him weak again."

"Oh, yeah?" said Larryboy.

"Yeah," the cherry tomato responded. "Think for a minute, Larryboy. Wouldn't you like to have a nice shield?"

"Sure, who wouldn't?" said the superhero. "But I am pretty happy with the stuff I do have, like these nifty super-suction ears."

"Yeah, but other heroes can fly. Wouldn't you like to be able to fly?"

"That would be fun. But you know what? I already fly with my Larry-Jet. So I'm okay with not being able to fly."

"Drat!" mumbled the Emperor.

"You've defeated envy!" Junior shouted.

"That's right, thanks to you," said Larryboy.

"But you haven't defeated *me* yet!" cried the Emperor. "Army, attack!"

"But, Emperor," Jesse whined, "he isn't weak anymore."

"I've got an idea," said Frank.

"What?" asked Jesse.

"Run!"

Frank and Jesse ran down the street. Larryboy aimed an ear towards them and *POP!* One of his super-suction ears flew down the street. The plunger zoomed past the two potatoes and landed on a billboard advertising Mister Slushee.

"Hah!" shouted Frank. "He missed!"

"You know," said Jesse, "the last time we thought he missed, he didn't really miss."

"What are you trying to say?" asked Frank.

"I guess I'm trying to say, 'Look out!'" hollered Jesse.

Larryboy reeled in his plunger, which uprooted the billboard and pulled it right toward the two henchmen.

WAP! The billboard and the henchmen collided. Frank and Jesse fell to the ground in a daze.

"That ought to keep them quiet for a little bit," said Larryboy. "And now for the ringleader!"

"I still have an ace up my sleeve!" said the Emperor.

"Hah!" crowed Larryboy. "You don't even have sleeves!"

"It's just an expression," said the Emperor. "Watch!"

The Emperor held his breath and nearly shrunk out of sight!

"Oh, no!" cried Junior. "He'll get away!"

"Don't worry," said Larryboy. "Archie thought the Emperor might try to use his super-shrinking power. That's why he packed this!"

Larryboy pulled a handheld Larry-Vacuum from his utility belt. He turned on the vacuum, which sucked dust and debris into its bag. After a minute, Larry turned the vacuum off.

"Now what?" asked Junior.

"Now we wait until the Emperor can't hold his breath anymore."

POOF!

Suddenly a bulge the size and shape of a cherry tomato appeared inside the vacuum bag.

"Looks like we caught the Emperor after all," said Larryboy.

"Thank you for saving the day, Larryboy!" said Junior.

"Thank you, Junior, for showing me how to defeat envy."

BRRRRRING!

"That would be for me," said Larryboy. "Hello, Archie?"

"Larryboy! Are you okay?"

"Thanks to Junior and you, I'm fine."

"And what about the Emperor?"

"Don't worry, Archie. I've got that one in the bag!"

CHAPTER 19

ALL'S WELL THAT ENDS

SKRITCH!

A really huge, super gigantic, massively gargantuan car jack was placed in the doorway of the Bank of Bumblyburg.

Several citizens were working the lever, returning the height of the building to its normal size. Chief Croswell, Junior, and Larryboy watched from down the street.

"Soon all of the buildings will be back to their normal sizes," said the chief. "And all of Bumblyburg's citizens have been examined by the doctor. All traces of the Envy Formula are gone!"

"That *is* good news," said Larryboy.

"We sure learned a good lesson, didn't we?" asked Junior.

"That's right," said Larryboy. "Don't mess with Larryboy!"

"Oh, I was thinking of a different lesson," said Junior.

"I know just what you're thinking," said

Larryboy. "Free Slushees aren't all they're cracked up to be."

"Uhm, that isn't it, either" said Junior.

"Don't throw a shield in a classroom?" suggested Larryboy.

"That's good advice," said Junior. "But still, it's not what I was thinking. What is the big thing we learned in this adventure?"

"The prison cots are lumpy?"

"I was thinking more along the lines of being content with what we have," sighed Junior.

"Right! That, too!" agreed the superhero, "Well, I must be off."

Larryboy hopped into his waiting Larry-Mobile. He fired up the engine and drove down the street. Chief Croswell and Junior waved.

As Larryboy came to a stop at the traffic light, a hotrod painted with yellow and red flames pulled up alongside him. The light changed, and the hotrod took off.

"Boy, it sure would be nice to have a car like that," Larryboy said to himself. "But then again, the car I've got isn't too bad!"

Larryboy laughed as he pushed the special button on his dashboard. Suddenly, wings popped out of the side of the Larry-Mobile. The car lifted up into the air, and Larryboy zoomed off into the sky.

SOFTCOVER ISBN 978-0-310-70468-3

CHAPTER 1

THE GIANT SLIME MONSTER

It was an average day in Bumblyburg. The leaves were rustling on the trees, the birds were perched on the statues in the park, and Bumblyburg's own superhero, Larryboy, was on patrol.

Larryboy was slowly driving the Larry-Mobile around the city, looking for signs of crime or other superhero-needing situations. Normally, Larryboy liked going on patrol. But today, he was bored.

"I am sooo bored!" he said. "There's nothing happening today … except for the situation with the birds and the statues. But I'm not going to intervene in that! If I don't see some sorta trouble soon, I'm gonna go home and make myself a big peanut-butter sandwi …"

The Larry-Mobile screeched to a halt. Larryboy saw something coming over the hill, and he couldn't believe his eyes.

A great big slimy purple blob was creeping over the hill, wiggling menacingly as it came.

"Oh, peanut brittle!" said Larryboy. "It's a giant purple slime monster!!"

Right then, Larryboy would have attacked the giant purple slime monster in an effort to save Bumblyburg from its vicious slimy attacks. He would have attacked, except for on thing: Larryboy was scared of giant purple slime monsters.

So instead, Larryboy parked the Larry-Mobile and jumped into the bushes to hide as the giant purple slime monster came over the hill.

"Bumblyburg is doomed!" Larryboy thought to himself. "We

need a superhero or something to stop it!"

Then, with horror, Larryboy realized something. "Wait … *I* … am … that … hero. Drat."

Even though he was afraid, he had to try to stop the giant purple slime monster. Bumblyburg depended on him!

So, as the giant purple slime monster passed the bushes where Larryboy was hiding, he closed his eyes, gritted his teeth, and fired one of his plunger ears.

"Hey!" said the giant purple slime monster. "I've been plungerized!"

This startled Larryboy. He didn't expect the giant purple slime monster to talk. Besides, it didn't sound *anything* like a giant purple slime monster should sound.

"Help! Get this plunger off me! I can't see!" it said.

Then Larryboy realized something: The giant purple slime monster didn't sound like a giant purple slime monster. It sounded like Wally!

Larryboy looked up from behind the bushes, and this is what he saw: Herbert and Wally carrying the largest plate of grape-flavored gelatin he had ever seen.

Larryboy rushed from the bushes and released Wally from his plunger ear. Herbert and Wally explained that they had filled the city swimming pool with grape gelatin, and now they were taking the whole thing home to eat. They didn't even seem to mind that there was a pair of swim fins and a life preserver suspended in the middle of the giant gelatin mold.

"Wow," said Larryboy. "That's a lot of gelatin!"

Also look for *Larryboy and the Sinister Snow Day* and *Larryboy and the Yodelnapper* coming spring 2003!